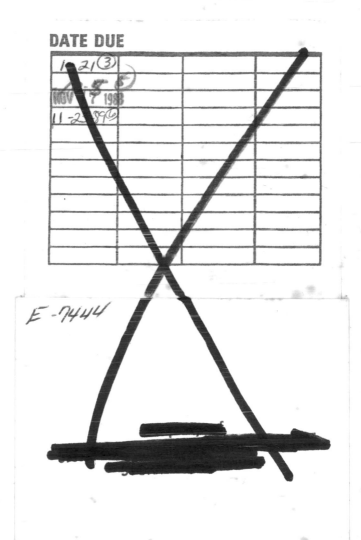

KIDS CAN'T STOP READING
THE CHOOSE YOUR
OWN ADVENTURE® STORIES!

CHOOSE YOUR OWN ADVENTURE®—
AND MAKE READING MORE FUN!

Bantam Books in the Choose Your Own Adventure™ Series
Ask your bookseller for the books you have missed

#1 THE CAVE OF TIME
#2 JOURNEY UNDER THE SEA
#3 BY BALLOON TO THE SAHARA
#4 SPACE AND BEYOND
#5 THE MYSTERY OF CHIMNEY ROCK
#6 YOUR CODE NAME IS JONAH
#7 THE THIRD PLANET FROM ALTAIR
#8 DEADWOOD CITY
#9 WHO KILLED HARLOWE THROMBEY?
#10 THE LOST JEWELS OF NABOOTI
#11 MYSTERY OF THE MAYA
#12 INSIDE UFO 54-40
#13 THE ABOMINABLE SNOWMAN
#14 THE FORBIDDEN CASTLE
#15 HOUSE OF DANGER
#16 SURVIVAL AT SEA
#17 THE RACE FOREVER
#18 UNDERGROUND KINGDOM
#19 SECRET OF THE PYRAMIDS
#20 ESCAPE
#21 HYPERSPACE
#22 SPACE PATROL
#23 THE LOST TRIBE
#24 LOST ON THE AMAZON
#25 PRISONER OF THE ANT PEOPLE
#26 THE PHANTOM SUBMARINE
#27 THE HORROR OF HIGH RIDGE

#28 MOUNTAIN SURVIVAL
#29 TROUBLE ON PLANET EARTH
#30 THE CURSE OF BATTERSLEA HALL
#31 VAMPIRE EXPRESS
#32 TREASURE DIVER
#33 THE DRAGONS' DEN
#34 THE MYSTERY OF THE HIGHLAND CREST
#35 JOURNEY TO STONEHENGE
#36 THE SECRET TREASURE OF TIBET
#37 WAR WITH THE EVIL POWER MASTER
#38 SABOTAGE
#39 SUPERCOMPUTER
#40 THE THRONE OF ZEUS
#41 SEARCH FOR THE MOUNTAIN GORILLAS
#42 THE MYSTERY OF ECHO LODGE
#43 GRAND CANYON ODYSSEY
#44 THE MYSTERY OF URA SENKE
#45 YOU ARE A SHARK
#46 THE DEADLY SHADOW
#47 OUTLAWS OF SHERWOOD FOREST
#48 SPY FOR GEORGE WASHINGTON
#49 DANGER AT ANCHOR MINE
#50 RETURN TO THE CAVE OF TIME
#51 THE MAGIC OF THE UNICORN
#52 GHOST HUNTER

GHOST HUNTER

BY EDWARD PACKARD

ILLUSTRATED BY TED ENIK

BANTAM BOOKS
TORONTO • NEW YORK • LONDON • SYDNEY • AUCKLAND

RL 4, IL age 10 and up

GHOST HUNTER

A Bantam Book / January 1986

CHOOSE YOUR OWN ADVENTURE® is a registered trademark of Bantam Books, Inc. Registered in U.S. Patent and Trademark Office and elsewhere.

Original conception of Edward Packard.

Front cover art by Bill Schmidt.

ISBN 0-553-25488-X

Published simultaneously in the United States and Canada

Bantam Books are published by Bantam Books, Inc. Its trademark, consisting of the words "Bantam Books" and the portrayal of a rooster, is Registered in U.S. Patent and Trademark Office and in other countries. Marca Registrada. Bantam Books, Inc., 666 Fifth Avenue, New York, New York 10103.

PRINTED IN THE UNITED STATES OF AMERICA

O   0 9 8 7 6 5 4 3

GHOST HUNTER

WARNING!!!

Do not read this book straight through from beginning to end! These pages contain many different adventures you can have as you hunt for ghosts. From time to time as you read along, you will be asked to make decisions and choices. Your choices may lead to success or disaster! The adventures you have will be the result of the choices you make. After you make a choice, follow the directions to see what happens to you next.

Think carefully before you make a move. Ghost hunting is a dangerous business. Do you have the wits and courage to survive? You're about to find out.

Good luck!

Ever since you solved the Harlowe Thrombey murder case, your services as a private detective have been much in demand. Harlowe Thrombey was one of the richest men in town, and it was a surprise when he called you in to help find out who was plotting against his life. Unfortunately, Thrombey was murdered the very night you began your investigation. His widow, Jane Thrombey, was a prime suspect, but you proved her innocence, and afterward she continued to live in their huge Victorian house until she died of a heart attack a few months ago.

You've enjoyed being a private detective, but lately you've been thinking about going into a new field. In fact, you've decided to become a ghost hunter!

What got you interested was a magazine article on the subject. The author said that in most cases a haunted house was once the scene of a murder. This fact tied in with some news you heard recently: After Jane Thrombey died a few months ago, a man named Howard Grimstone bought the Thrombey place. Neighbors say that strange things have been going on there—lights on late at night, guard dogs patrolling the grounds, weird sounds coming from the house. The more you think about it, the more likely it seems that the ghost of Harlowe Thrombey has come to haunt the house where Thrombey was murdered.

Turn to page 2.

Another thing in the article caught your eye. The article said that Professor Zieback, who is supposed to be one of the world's leading authorities on ghosts, works at the Institute for Occult Studies only a few miles from where you live. The author did not seem to have a high opinion of Dr. Zieback, however. In fact, he said this:

Although Dr. Zieback has interviewed hundreds of people who claim to have seen ghosts, he admits he has never seen a ghost himself. How can he be so sure, then, that ghosts really exist? Doesn't he know that people have a way of seeing what they want to see or what they are afraid of seeing? Dr. Zieback's "evidence" for the existence of ghosts seems no more convincing than all the so-called evidence for UFOs and ESP.

You ask various people if they know anything about Dr. Zieback. A neighbor of yours, Mrs. Walecka, tells you that she's known Dr. Zieback for many years. "I don't know whether his theories about ghosts are true or not, but I do know this," she says. "He is an honest man."

You wonder whether it would be useful to see Dr. Zieback or not.

If you decide to pay a call on Professor Zieback, turn to page 4.

If you decide to start ghost hunting without delay, turn to page 11.

Back home, you think about what's happened. You've managed to lose a small fortune in diamonds that belong to an innocent woman who asked for your help. Your only consoling thought is that they are lying in the grass. Maybe someday you can get them back.

If you call the police and tell them everything, turn to page 22.

If you decide to think more about what to do, turn to page 7.

4

Within the hour you knock on the door of Professor Zieback's office at the Institute. A moment later you are greeted by a tall, slim man wearing a tweed vest and polka-dot bow tie. He ushers you into a tiny office, which is made even smaller by huge stacks of books piled up against the walls.

"Sit down and make yourself comfortable." The professor taps the ashes out of his pipe and stuffs in some tobacco, but, evidently deciding you might not want to sit in a room full of smoke, he lays the pipe down on his already cluttered desk. "What can I do for you? I'm sorry, but I have to go to a meeting and I only have a few minutes."

"Well," you say, clearing your throat, "I read that you've done a lot of research on ghosts. I thought maybe you could give me a few tips."

Turn to page 6.

6

"Tips?" The professor frowns. "Well, it's a very complicated subject, not one that boils down to a few *tips*. That being said, I will tell you this. Number one: Ghosts exist, but they normally don't exist in a way in which we are aware of their existence, so most of the time it doesn't matter whether they exist or not."

"I don't quite follow—" you start to say, but the professor interrupts you with an upraised finger.

"I'm not surprised you *can't* follow—it's very complicated, as I say. *But* what I say next you can follow. Number two: Ghosts *don't* hurt people. You are more likely to be hurt if you run from a ghost than if you go toward it."

The professor takes a gold watch out of his pocket and looks at it. "Oops, I'm very late!"

As he gets to his feet and grabs his jacket from the coat stand, he waves his pipe at you. "Goodbye. I wish you luck. Good day."

Before you can even thank the professor, he's out the door. You glance around the cluttered little office a moment and then head for home, thinking about what he said.

Turn to page 11.

That evening you're sitting at your desk still wondering what to do. You've just about decided to call the police and tell them everything you know, but you feel embarrassed about not having called already. You pace around restlessly, then sit on the couch, thinking. You doze off.

Your next sensation is that of a presence in the room, an unearthly presence. Half opening your eyes, you confront a blurred outline—as if the figure before you were fashioned out of fog condensed into human shape. Uncertain as the image is, you recognize it, and the shock of recognition freezes you. You grab the back of the couch and the armrest for support. Standing at the far side of the room is the ghost of Harlowe Thrombey!

Turn to page 21.

"I'm sorry, I just don't think I can help," you say.

"Well, thanks for your time. I guess there isn't anything to be done."

After Sylvia leaves, you go for a walk to think things over. By the time you get home you've decided that you really should try to help Sylvia. It's not right that she should be deprived of her rightful inheritance.

The next morning you call her, but there is no answer. Every day you try again, but it's a week before you're able to reach her.

"Oh, it's you!" she says. "I should have let you know I was visiting my mother. I got back yesterday and found out that Grimstone has left town. The place is all locked up."

"Why do you think he cleared out?"

"The police have been watching the place. He may have figured they had gotten enough evidence against him to close in on him."

"Maybe so," you reply. "It also may mean that he found the diamonds." A thought suddenly occurs to you. "Could you get a court order to have the place searched?"

"I already tried," Sylvia replies. "The judge denied my request. He said that there wasn't enough evidence to justify his issuing a search warrant."

"Well, maybe I can think of something."

Go on to the next page.

Sitting at your desk with your feet propped up in your best thinking position, you wonder what to do next. Somehow you've got to get inside the house.

That afternoon you walk halfway across town—to the section where most of the rich people live—and stand across the street from the great white house where Harlowe Thrombey was murdered. The grounds are surrounded by a wrought-iron fence that's too high to climb except at the front gate. You glance at the man sitting in an old car parked in front of the house. You've been in the detective business long enough to know a plainclothes policeman when you see one.

Maybe you should get Jenny to help. She could distract the policeman while you find a way to climb over the fence. On the other hand, you don't like the idea of sneaking into a place that's guarded by the police. Maybe you should join Jenny in investigating the Gray mansion.

If you call Jenny and ask for her help, turn to page 68.

If you call Jenny and offer to help her, turn to page 14.

10

You've come this far, and you don't intend to leave without those diamonds! Jiggling your flashlight to get enough light to see by, you open the cedar closet and go back to the right rear corner. You stand the flashlight on end while you pry away at the wall paneling with your pocketknife.

In a minute a panel comes loose. You pry it off and reach for the flashlight to shine it in the hole in the wall. There you see a small box covered in red leather. You've found the diamonds!

Turn to page 19.

You're sitting at your desk thinking about how you might begin your work as a ghost hunter when the phone rings. It's your old friend Jenny Mudge. That's quite a coincidence! Jenny, who is also a private detective, helped you solve the Harlowe Thrombey murder case!

"How are things?" you ask.

Jenny replies in her usual lively voice. "Very fine. I've stopped being a private detective and decided to become a ghost hunter!"

"That's amazing," you say. "Great minds think alike! I was just about to see if I can find out whether Harlowe Thrombey's ghost has returned to haunt his old house."

"Could be," Jenny replies. "But *I've* learned of a house that by all reports is *definitely* haunted. It's just a little way out of town—the Gray mansion. It's been empty for a long time. The place is so haunted, weird, cursed—whatever you want to call it—that no one will go near it. I called you to see if you'd like to go out there with me this Saturday."

If you decide to join Jenny, turn to page 14.

If you decide to hunt for Harlowe Thrombey's ghost instead, turn to page 18.

Keeping a wary eye on the landing above, you continue up the stairs. There is no further sign of a ghost, but as you reach the top step your flashlight flickers out. You bang it on the floor and it flickers on. With your flashlight flickering on and off, you feel your way along the wall.

You reach a door, open it, and shine your light around a large walk-in closet. From the distinctive smell of cedar, you can tell you've reached the right place.

Suddenly there is a sound behind you!

Whirling around, you feel a sack drawn down over your head. You scream and try to bite the strong hands that are binding ropes tightly around your arms. You struggle to wrench free, but you're tackled and dropped to the floor. You feel ropes being pulled tight around your legs. Your attacker rolls you along the attic floor, and you come to rest up against a wall with a *thunk*.

For a moment you're afraid you'll suffocate, but then you realize the sack is made of burlap. Enough air gets through for you to breathe.

"What's going on?" you hear a man exclaim. The sound of his footsteps is becoming louder. Suddenly he screams. You hear him moving away. *"No, no, don't come near me!"*

Why is he yelling?

Turn to page 32.

When you arrive at Jenny's house on Saturday, she greets you excitedly. "The Gray mansion is still empty," she says.

"Then what are we waiting for?" you reply.

"Nothing, now that I've found my flashlight," Jenny answers.

There is a light drizzle falling and the sky has an oppressive, leaden look when you reach the top of a hill and look up at the huge Tudor house. Its turrets lean and its porches sag from decades of neglect.

The massive front door is bolted shut, but halfway around the house you find an unlocked door that leads to a butler's pantry. You've hardly reached the somber, musty hallway when you hear a wailing, moaning sound that rises and falls in pitch, over and over.

"This way," Jenny says, her voice a little shaky.

You follow her into a large room with massive oak tables and chests, and chairs covered with dark brown leather. Your eyes fix on the great stone fireplace. The wailing sound is louder now—and it's coming straight from the fireplace.

Go on to the next page.

"Maybe it's only the wind," you say.

Jenny clutches your arm tightly. "The wind never sounds like that."

"Then I guess it's a ghost."

Jenny places her mouth close to your ear. "If we're going to trap it, we have to surround it. One of us must go up on the roof and shine the flashlight down the chimney while the other watches the fireplace."

"How can we get up on the roof?"

"I noticed an upstairs porch on the left side of the house," Jenny answers. "It wouldn't be hard to swing onto the roof from there. Do you want to try it, or shall I?"

If you say you'll go up on the roof, turn to page 41.

If you decide to stay by the chimney, turn to page 55.

Blinking, you turn on more lights, but there is no trace of any presence in the room. Were you dreaming? It seemed so real!

You walk outside and look at the waning moon. You feel certain that, in some way, you will be helped by Harlowe Thrombey's ghost.

You pick up the phone and call Sylvia Ruston. "I think I can get your diamonds, but I'll have to turn them over to the police first, you know. You'll have to prove they belong to you and not to Grimstone."

"That will be no trouble," Sylvia replies. "Thank you—I'd almost given up hope. And I promise you'll be well paid if you succeed."

The next evening at seven you walk up to the gate of Grimstone's house. There are now four attack dogs, and they are all loose on the grounds. The two who attacked you before remember your scent. They run up and down the inside of the fence, raging and growling.

You ring the buzzer at the gate. In a moment Kenny appears. "I can help Mr. Grimstone with his problem," you say.

Kenny commands the dogs to return to their pen, locks them in, and respectfully ushers you down the front walk and into the house. You wonder at his change of attitude. Perhaps Harlowe Thrombey's ghost has been at work!

Turn to page 24.

You decide, first of all, to pay a call on Howard Grimstone, the new owner of the Thrombey house. You're sitting at your desk thinking about what to ask him when a woman appears at your front door.

"I'm Sylvia Ruston, Jane Thrombey's niece," she says. "May I come in?"

"Of course."

You take a close look at your visitor as you usher her into your office. She is a rather plump, round-faced woman—in her forties, you'd guess. Her skin is so fair you imagine she must sunburn very easily. Her yellowish hair is curly. She looks as if she has a basically happy nature, but right now she seems tense and anxious. You had heard that Jane Thrombey had left most of her money to Sylvia, and you're curious to know what brought her to see you.

"Sit down . . . What seems to be the problem?" You motion her toward the old couch next to your desk.

"I'm penniless, and I should be rich."

You search Sylvia's eyes for a clue to her character. "What do you mean? I heard you inherited most of your Aunt Jane's wealth—everything except the house."

Turn to page 26.

As you reach for the box, you sense a presence behind you. You half turn around to look. This time it's not a sack coming down over your head but the steel barrel of an automatic rifle—the last thing you ever see.

The End

This case is getting very interesting. Whom should you work for—Sylvia Ruston or Howard Grimstone? It wouldn't seem right to work for both of them without telling them what you're doing. Yet that doesn't make sense.

You'd be more inclined to work for Grimstone—you want to be a ghost hunter. On the other hand, you don't like the idea of working for a criminal. Still, Grimstone isn't asking you to do anything illegal, so why not take the case? Yet you feel some loyalty to Sylvia Ruston because she came to you first.

You can't just let your thoughts go around in circles like this. You've got to make a decision!

*If you decide to work for Sylvia Ruston,
turn to page 28.*

*If you decide to work for Howard Grimstone,
turn to page 70.*

"Why are you here? What do you want?" you blurt out.

"Do not be afraid," the ghost replies. "You will come to no harm. But you should not be surprised to be haunted by me: I hired you to save my life, and yet I was murdered that very night."

"I wish I could have saved you, but at least I found out who murdered you."

"Yes," the ghost acknowledges, "but it is your fate to be haunted by me."

"Shouldn't you be haunting your old house?" you ask.

"I have spent many hours there," says Thrombey. "I do not like to see my house possessed by an evil man."

"Then why don't you do something about it?" you demand.

"It is the way of ghosts not to punish evil people, but to let them bring about their own downfall. That gives people like you a chance to be a good force in the world."

"But I'm no match for Grimstone and his thugs," you say, "unless . . . Would you help me?"

"If you are brave enough to try, then your courage should be rewarded." With these words, the ghost vanishes.

Turn to page 17.
E-1444

Within a few minutes after you phone the police, two detectives arrive at your house. They are very interested in your story about the diamonds, and even more so about the weapons and explosives. They ask you to sign a statement about what you saw.

Grimstone's house is put under police surveillance. A couple of days later the state police and the FBI raid the house and break up one of the most dangerous arms-smuggling groups in America, confiscating enough weapons and explosives to start a small war.

The next day, you lead the two detectives and the clerk of the probate court to the tree where you lost the diamonds while escaping from Grimstone's attack dogs. The clerk holds a tray, and the detectives watch while you run your fingers through the grass and look for sparkles of light. Each time you find a diamond, you drop it onto the tray. No one talks, except when you brush aside a wet leaf and expose the magnificent Khartoum Star.

The younger detective gasps.

"The biggest I ever saw," says the other.

A few minutes later the clerk announces, "Thirty-seven. Looks as if you got them all!"

"Thanks for your help," the older detective says. "We'll give you a lift home."

Turn to page 47.

By making a tremendous effort you're able to get to your feet, then hobble around, twisting and turning. You can feel the ropes beginning to work loose. You keep struggling. You have to rest every once in a while—breathing is difficult through the burlap bag. At last you work one hand free, then the other. In a few moments you're able to pull the bag up over your head. You work the ropes loose from around your legs. You're sore, bruised, and exhausted, but you're free!

Stumbling around in the dark, you kick something—the flashlight! You pick it up. It still doesn't work right. But at least it flickers on when you shake it.

Then you hear a voice groaning at the bottom of the stairs. The man who attacked you must be regaining consciousness.

If you go into the cedar closet and try to find the diamonds, turn to page 10.

If you try to get out of the house right away, turn to page 33.

Grimstone is waiting for you in the library. Two of his henchmen are standing, arms folded, backs to the wall, watching, like vultures perched in a tree.

"Okay," says Grimstone, "where are the diamonds?"

"What diamonds?" you quickly reply.

The men move closer, but Grimstone stops them with a wave of his hand.

"Don't play coy with me. We found out where they were hidden, and we know you got away with them. Do you think I would have let you back in this house if I didn't know you had the diamonds?"

"I thought you wanted me to help catch ghosts!"

"There *are* no ghosts," Grimstone sneers at you. "I made up that story to get you over here. I even had ghost effects to entertain you. I thought you'd give away the location of the diamonds. You outsmarted me for awhile, but now . . ."

At a glance from Grimstone, the thugs move closer. One of them unsheathes a knife and holds the sharp edge next to your throat.

"Where—are—the—diamonds?" Grimstone repeats, thrusting his face close to yours.

---

*If you tell where the diamonds are,
turn to page 54.*

*If you try to talk your way out of it,
turn to page 107.*

Sylvia leans toward you. "Aunt Jane provided in her will that the house and furniture be sold and the proceeds given to charity. All her money and jewels were to be left to me. But before she died she put her money into diamonds. She even told me how many. There were thirty-seven. One of them was the famous Khartoum Star—one of the largest diamonds in the world! She hid them in a red leather box, and I'm the only one who knows it. The house has been sold, but I'm sure the diamonds are still in it. In fact, I think I know exactly where they are. Aunt Jane once showed me her secret hiding place—behind a wood panel in the right rear corner of the cedar closet in the attic."

"What do you know about Howard Grimstone, the new owner?"

"Not much," Sylvia replies with a shrug. "But there are a lot of rumors about him. I've heard he's a big drug dealer. There's also a rumor that he's in the arms-smuggling business and that he makes bombs for terrorists."

"Not the kind of man you could ask to help you look for your diamonds, I guess."

By now you can see that this is going to be a tricky case, and it will delay your new career as a ghost hunter. Besides, you're not really sure you can help.

If you tell Sylvia you don't think you can help her, turn to page 8.

If you tell her you'll think about it, turn to page 34.

"It's the strangest thing," Grimstone begins, in what strikes you as a rather phony tone of voice. "I recently bought a house owned by Jane Thrombey, who died a few months ago. It's a great house—suits my needs in every way—but it has one problem." Grimstone leans forward as if to add emphasis to his statement.

"And what's the problem?"

"Ghosts! The place is haunted. Strange wailing sounds and lights—my employees and I can't get a good night's sleep! That's bad enough. But other things have been happening. Last night the crystal chandelier began swaying wildly. Then some of the crystals crashed onto the dining-room table. One of my men was cut by flying glass. I've never believed in ghosts before, but I'm telling you there's one in that house!"

"What do you want me to do?"

Grimstone leans forward. His thin lips stretch into some sort of a smile. "I need someone to find that ghost and get rid of it. I need a ghost hunter!"

"I'll think about it and let you know in the morning," you say.

As he leaves, Grimstone turns. "I'll make it worth your while."

Turn to page 20.

You call Sylvia Ruston, and she agrees to come over right away. While waiting for her to arrive, you turn over in your mind this problem: If you ask Grimstone to let you look for the diamonds, won't you be at his mercy once he sees where they are?

When Sylvia arrives, a discouraged look on her face, you don't have a chance to explain your thinking before she begins talking a mile a minute.

"The more I think about this, the more hopeless it seems," she begins. "If I can't get a court order, I don't see how we can get those diamonds. It's not as if we're trying to catch Grimstone doing something wrong. He's not stealing the diamonds—he doesn't even know they're in his house."

"I agree," you say. "I think the only thing to do is to confront Grimstone—tell him we know where the diamonds are and can lead him to them. Then we'll jointly turn them over to the police. Based on what you've told me, I feel confident that any court would rule that you are their rightful owner."

Go on to the next page.

"But you're acting as if Grimstone can be trusted," Sylvia protests. "As soon as we show him the diamonds, he might very well kill us! At the very least he'll pocket them all and claim we made up the story to blackmail him."

"You have a good point," you reply, "but I've been thinking about this problem—I think I have a way around it. Before we go to Grimstone's house, I'll mail letters to the police telling them what we're about to do. We'll be able to warn Grimstone that if anything happens to us, the police will know exactly who is responsible!"

"It still sounds risky," Sylvia says, "but I'm willing to try it."

Turn to page 42.

You're dead—dead as far as any human would say. But you aren't dead from *your* standpoint, because you can feel yourself floating, drifting into a house—passing like television waves through walls and doors and floors, your image invisible. Floating and not always silent, but like a sometimes moaning, sometimes howling, wind that whips through trees, rattles windows, and sends shafts of air past flickering candles, your presence hovers through time. Then it moves and is felt.

Live people—solid people—walk, run, and stumble. One gasps, another screams: terror in their eyes, their chests tight, panting, gripped by fear. The ghost that haunts them is *you*.

The End

You hear another scream. Then a series of noises that sound like someone falling down the stairs. Then silence.

You wriggle to get free, but you can hardly move. Whoever tied you up knew what he was doing.

"You're giving up?" You recognize the voice of Harlowe Thrombey's ghost!

"Why did you do this to me? Let me go!" you cry.

"I didn't do this," the ghost says. "A living person did it—a petty criminal who works for Howard Grimstone and thought he would get a little something for himself."

"What happened to him? Did you push him down the stairs?"

"No," the ghost replies patiently. "He was so frightened he fell down the stairs. He's unconscious now, but he's not badly hurt."

"Well I'm glad he's out cold. Now, could you please let me loose?"

Again the ghost laughs—that same laugh that frightened you on the stairs. "You don't understand. Ghosts do not hurt people. Nor do they help them, though—as you can see—people are often hurt or helped in the presence of ghosts."

You start to ask another question, but there is no reply.

Turn to page 23.

Keeping as quiet as you can, you hurry down the stairs. You hear more groaning. Your flickering flashlight shines on a brute of a man lying on the floor at the bottom of the attic stairs. He opens one eye. He's coming to! Beyond him on the floor is an automatic rifle!

You jump over the man, grab the rifle, and run down the stairs. In a moment you're at the front door. The man yells from upstairs.

"I'll get you!"

You fumble with the latch as you hear him charging after you.

At last you get the door open. You slam it shut behind you and run toward the gate, yelling, *"Help! Police!"*

The unmarked police car swings around, training its headlights on you. A man jumps out, revolver in hand

"Drop that rifle!"

"There's a dangerous man in there," you shout as you toss the rifle aside.

"Wait on the other side of the car. Keep down!"

The cop ducks behind a tree and draws a bead on the front door.

On the other side of the car you find Jenny Mudge. "Glad you made it!" she says. "I was worried about you. You were in there so long, I finally told the policeman. More cops are on the way— they were going to search the house!"

Turn to page 52.

After Sylvia Ruston leaves, you sit at your desk wondering how you can possibly help her. If you take the case, you'll hardly be able to call up Grimstone and ask if you can search a closet in his attic. If you were to tell him what you are looking for, the diamonds would surely vanish by the time you got there.

You tilt back, feet on your desk, eyes closed. A loud knocking interrupts your thoughts. Opening the door, you find a rather short, stocky man. His oily graying hair is slicked back over his head. A close-shaven mustache looks like a line of greasepaint over his thin, almost nonexistent, upper lip.

"I'm Howard Grimstone. I've heard you're a private detective—and I need your help!"

You try to hide your astonishment. "Well, please come in." You motion to the same old couch Sylvia Ruston so recently vacated. "What's your problem?"

Turn to page 27.

"I don't think ghosts hurt anyone," you whisper to Jenny. "They just scare people. Besides, how can we hunt a ghost if we're always running?"

Jenny grips your belt, and the two of you start up the stairs step by step. You close your eyes a moment, hoping the ghost will go away, but it doesn't. It seems to become more and more solid. You can see the lines etched in its face. Its hollow dark eyes seem to be tunnels to nowhere.

You can read the expression on its face. You feel as if it's deciding what to do to you. Jenny is still clutching your belt. You take another step, but you're really not thinking.

The laughter of the ghost rings in your ears.

Your eyes are focused on your feet, which feel increasingly heavier—as if they are about to become rooted.

When you look up, the ghost is only two steps above you. It seems huge.

"Jenny," you whisper hoarsely, "it's not solid. We can make it."

Pulling Jenny by the hand, you step up to the ghost—*and through it!*

Turn to page 48.

You slip the diamonds into your pockets, close the leather box, and replace the wood panel. You quietly shut the closet door and tiptoe down the attic stairs. You hope your bulging pockets aren't too noticeable! As you come down the back stairs, you hear laughter coming from the dining room. Grimstone's henchmen seem occupied with their drinking and poker-playing.

Myra is waiting, nervously sipping a cup of tea.

"I think I'd better leave now," you say.

"And I'm leaving the day after tomorrow," says Myra, "as soon as Mr. Grimstone gets back."

"Are you going to tell the police about the weapons?"

Myra shakes her head. "If I do, they'll investigate. He'll know I told and he'll kill me. I know it—he warned me. And please don't you tell them, either. Otherwise, you may be responsible for my death."

"Then why did you show me that room?"

Myra's voice trembles as she answers. "Because if anything happens to me, I want someone to know."

Suddenly you remember the diamonds bulging in your pockets. Sooner or later Kenny and his friends will come out of the dining room—if only for more beer from the refrigerator.

"I have to leave, Myra. Please keep in touch with me!"

"Goodbye," Myra whispers.

Go on to the next page.

Careful to make no noise, you open the back door and pause to look and listen. All is quiet. The almost-full moon is flickering through the branches of the big oak trees that decorate the yard. Cautiously you step forward. You've got about fifty yards to go to make it to the front gate.

One of the big dogs races across the lawn. You freeze. The dog disappears around the back of the house. Probably chasing a squirrel or a stray cat, you think.

From behind you, standing at the open door, Myra whispers, "They've let the dogs out for the night!"

"I know!" you whisper back. "Can I hide in the house overnight?"

"It's all right with me, but I hope the men don't find you," Myra answers.

If you decide to hide in the house overnight, turn to page 44.

If you decide to try to make it past the dogs, turn to page 98.

Leaving Jenny to watch the fireplace, you climb the broad central staircase. In the second-floor hall you find a door leading to an upstairs porch. You are able to pivot around the corner post of the porch railing out onto the roof. Though you have a good tread on your sneakers and the roof is not steeply pitched, the slate shingles are wet and slippery, and you have to work your way up with great care. You're beginning to feel more afraid of falling than of coming face to face with the ghost!

About halfway up the chimney, you pass the attic window. Looking into it you see a face—a pale gray face with a twisted shadow of a mouth and great hollow eyes! Instinctively you rear back—only a few inches, but enough to lose your balance! Desperately you drop to your hands and knees to try to get traction on the roof, but it's too late. You're falling, tumbling, head over heels over the edge.

Your neck twists as your head hits the hard ground.

Turn to page 30.

When Sylvia calls Howard Grimstone and tells him that she and you know of the secret location of some jewels in his house, he immediately invites you both over.

Approaching the imposing mansion, you cast an anxious eye on the dog pen attached to the house. Two huge mastiffs lunge up against the chain-link fence as if they are ready to tear you to bits.

Howard Grimstone, his piercing dark eyes watching your approach, is waiting, smiling, at the door. "Please come in," he says, and leads you and Sylvia into the sumptuous house where Harlowe Thrombey lived and died. Behind Grimstone is a hulking thug of a man with a crew cut and a flat unhealthy looking face.

"It's all right, Kenny," Grimstone says to the thug, who slips into the shadows.

Grimstone then turns to greet you as if you were long-lost friends.

"Of course if there are diamonds hidden here, we shall turn them over to the authorities," he says, "and if the court rules they belong to you, Miss Ruston, I shall be the first to congratulate you."

Go on to the next page.

You're suspicious of Grimstone's oily smoothness. While he talks, you cast your eyes at the expensive wood paneling and the heavy oak furniture that couldn't be bought in ordinary stores. Harlowe Thrombey certainly lived in the grand manner, you reflect. Still, you wouldn't want to live in a place like this, even if you were a millionaire—it's too dark and gloomy.

"Well," says Grimstone after a long pause. "Where *are* the diamonds?"

"In the attic," Sylvia replies.

"Well then," Grimstone says, "follow me."

Grimstone leads the way, followed by Sylvia, then you, and then Kenny, up the three flights to the attic. As you approach the cedar closet, you get ready to say the words that may be necessary to save your life—for you are by now convinced that Grimstone might kill you and Sylvia as soon as he learns the location of the jewels.

"So it's here, then," Grimstone says, as you stop before the door to the cedar closet.

At that moment you turn around and face him. "You should know, Mr. Grimstone, that a letter is already in the mail. The police will receive it tomorrow. It says that if I don't call them within two days, it will mean that harm has come to me at your hands."

Grimstone looks at you menacingly. His voice is filled with sarcasm. "What a rude thing to say! You don't deserve my hospitality after that. Now, show us the diamonds!"

Turn to page 58.

"I'm not going to try to get past those dogs," you tell Myra. "I've got to hide here until they're back in their pen."

Myra glances around nervously at the door to the dining room. You realize that she, as well as you, could be in bad trouble if Grimstone's men came in right now.

She touches your shoulder and gestures. "There—in the laundry room. I don't think they'll look in there."

She opens a door and flicks on the light. You duck inside. The tiny room is lined with a washer and dryer on one side and a long table at the other side. At the far end is a small window.

There's nothing to do but wait until the coast is clear. You switch off the light and stretch out on the table. With a stack of folded towels for a pillow, you settle down for a nap.

You sleep more soundly than you planned. When you wake up, the moon is high in the sky, casting a band of pale yellow light on the floor under the window. Suddenly you sit bolt upright. Standing on the washing machine is a fuzzy white image you instantly recognize. It is a man who is no longer a man—the ghost of Harlowe Thrombey!

Turn to page 49.

You wait in the library for what seems like a long time. Finally you step out into the hall, intent on going to the dining room and seeing what Grimstone is doing. Suddenly you hear a low-pitched sound, like a chord played on an organ. It swells in volume. The lights flicker and grow dim. At the end of the hallway a fuzzy, white light is glowing. Screwing up your courage, you step closer. The light becomes so intense you have to shield your eyes.

You step back. At that instant the light goes out; it's pitch-black. Strong hands seize your neck from behind. You scream and try to wriggle free. The hands thrust out violently, and you reel, striking your head against the wall as you go down.

You sit there dazed, trying to remember who you are, trying to get your wits about you. The lights come on. The door opens. Grimstone is there.

"Did you see it?" he cries. "It was in the dining room."

"It was out here," you say. "It was a—"

"It was even worse in the dining room!" Grimstone interrupts. "Do you think you can track it down? You can go anywhere you want."

"It might have come down the stairs," you say. "I'll check up there."

Turn to page 50.

During the days ahead, you wait eagerly to see what the probate judge will decide to do with the diamonds. In fact, you are called to testify at the hearing the following week.

The court rules that the diamonds belonged to Jane Thrombey and, therefore, awards them all to Sylvia Ruston in accordance with Jane Thrombey's will.

At the hearing, the judge says this to you: "You used poor judgment in going back to the house and in taking the diamonds. On the other hand, you showed courage in a perilous situation, and good judgment in calling the police when you did. You helped bring one of the worst criminals in America to justice. Congratulations. You have a great future."

The End

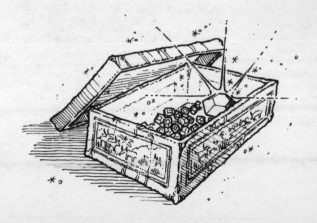

You crash into the door. You push it again with strength you never knew you had. The door flies open. You and Jenny run into the hallway—and toward the front of the house. Jenny throws open the front door. A fresh breeze blows in.

Looking back, you see only the dark empty hallway. You follow Jenny outside and slam the door behind you.

"What happened to the ghost?" Jenny asks. She's still shaking, and so are you.

"It just vanished," you reply. "Terrible as it was, it couldn't stand up to us."

"I guess we're pretty good ghost hunters," Jenny says.

"Good enough so that I think we won't have to hunt them any more."

"And somehow I don't think ghosts will be hunting us," says Jenny.

The End

"Why? How?" you blurt out.

Though you cannot see his lips move, you hear the voice you remember. "I am here because you are in my house, and you should remember that I died within hours after I asked you to save my life."

"I did my best! I solved the crime!" you reply.

"That hardly mattered to me—I died. And it is your destiny to be haunted by me."

"That's all very well," you say boldly, "but maybe you ought to haunt the criminals living in this house—and those vicious dogs, too."

There is a great swirl of gray light as the ghost rises into the air. It moves with increasing speed, circling the tiny room so fast that it seems to be everywhere at once. Then suddenly it's gone.

You get up off the table and wipe your brow. You're glad you still have your sanity! You open the door and peek into the dimly lighted kitchen. Suddenly you hear screams from the dining room. A man is yelling, "It's a ghost! Get away! NO! NO! NO! AHHHH!"

Smiling, you head down the main hall. Harlowe Thrombey's ghost is at work! You hear the dogs whimpering. They, too, must have been frightened by the ghost.

This is your chance. You run down the hall, push open the front door, and dash for the gate. In a few seconds you're over the top and safe on the other side, racing for home. Your pockets are still bulging with diamonds!

Turn to page 102.

As you walk cautiously up the stairs, you have an ominous feeling that what happened was not caused by a ghost. There was a fake note in Grimstone's voice, as if he'd rehearsed his lines to you. And how did he know "it was even worse in the dining room"?

As you reach a landing halfway up the stairs, you hear a deep, hollow voice. It seems to come from all around you.

"Are you ready to die? Are you? Are you?" the voice demands.

"No!" you shout. "Who are you? Where are you?"

"Ghosts are nowhere and everywhere," the voice replies. "Now find the diamonds and you shall be spared."

"What diamonds?" you say. Some instinct warns you not to admit how much you know.

"Find the diamonds or prepare to die," the voice repeats in an icy tone.

At this point you decide that whether this voice is a ghost or not, you'd better do what it says. You start up the steps to the attic. You sense that eyes are watching you. When you reach the top, you pause for a moment.

The voice is still nearby—and all around you. "Keep going. Find the diamonds."

Go on to the next page.

Desperately you try to think what to do as you continue through the dimly lighted attic. You pass near a small window that's already partly open. It looks like about a seven-foot drop to a slanting roof.

You could work your way down the roof and then jump. The dense shrubbery near the house should cushion your fall.

If you try to escape out the window, turn to page 108.

If you look through the attic until you find the cedar closet, turn to page 96.

If you just run back downstairs, turn to page 113.

In a moment you hear sirens. Two patrol cars arrive on the scene.

Spotlighted by a half dozen beams trained on the front door, your assailant comes out of the house, hands in the air. Later you confront him at police headquarters. The police identify their prisoner as Herman Nagar, a professional criminal wanted for bank robbery. Handcuffed and wearing a white bandage around his head, Nagar sits at a small steel table, flanked by two officers.

Chief Ludhorn, half sitting on the edge of his desk, removes an unlighted cigar from his mouth and eyes his prisoner.

"You know as well as I do, Nagar, of your right to a lawyer and your right to be silent."

Nagar grunts. "Get on with it."

Ludhorn scowls. "First of all, what were you doing in the house?"

"You know as well as I do, Chief. I worked for Grimstone. The heat was really on him, and we all cleared out of the house. There had been talk of diamonds hidden there, and I came back to try to find them—simple as that."

"Simple as that, plus attempted murder," the Chief says dryly.

Turn to page 63.

"Okay, okay," you blurt out. "I'll tell you. Just get that knife away."

"That's better." Grimstone motions his assistants to back off.

You lead Grimstone and the others out to the tree where you lost the diamonds. While Grimstone and you watch, his men crawl around, yelping with delight whenever they find one of the sparkling gems. Soon they can't find any more.

"Do you think they have them all?" Grimstone asks you.

"I think so."

"Then you're free to go. Show us how you climbed the tree and dropped over the fence. Just keep completely quiet and you'll be as safe as you were before you met me. But if you talk, we'll learn about it, and then it will be lights out for you."

Without bothering to answer, you leap up and grab a branch.

"Here come the dogs!" Kenny jeers.

But you're already up the tree and over the fence.

Back home, you decide that it's definitely time to talk to the police. You call Chief Ludhorn and tell him the whole story. At his suggestion you arrange to stay with a cousin who lives several hundred miles away until Grimstone's gang is broken up. A few days later Chief Ludhorn calls to tell you that Grimstone was shot by one of his own henchmen. "Can you imagine," the chief exclaims, "the murderer claims he thought he was shooting at a ghost!"

The End

You stand by the fireplace, ready to capture the ghost if Jenny scares it out. The wailing and moaning have stopped, and you wonder if it's because the ghost knows you are tracking it down. Perhaps it's like a wild animal that—once it knows it is being stalked—freezes and waits, ready to fight or flee if its adversary comes upon it.

Very slowly you inch toward the fireplace. You bend down to look up the chimney. As you stoop, your eye catches a painting on the wall— one of those portraits that is painted so that the eyes seem to follow you wherever you move.

You stop, hypnotized by those eyes. You wonder if you are looking at a painting of a man whose ghost now haunts his house. You shiver as the chill air coming down the chimney seems to wrap around you.

Suddenly a scream—from Jenny, up on the roof! *"It's in the attic! I've got to get down! I almost fell!"*

If you run to the upstairs porch to see if you can help Jenny, turn to page 79.

If you run upstairs to the attic, turn to page 60.

Shortly after sunset that evening, you climb over the iron gate in front of Grimstone's house and drop noiselessly to the ground. Fortunately the wind is blowing toward you, away from the dog pen; they're not likely to get your scent.

You carefully make your way around toward the kitchen. The blinds are drawn, but you can hear the muffled sound of laughter as you pass the dining room.

Myra is waiting for you. She lets you in the back door.

"Follow me," she whispers. "We mustn't let them hear us!"

You tiptoe behind her as she leads you up the back staircase to the second floor, then along a hallway, stopping in front of a closed door.

"Mr. Grimstone has always kept this door locked," she says, "but this time he forgot. Look inside!"

Myra opens the door and flips on a light. You stare open-mouthed at a row of open wooden crates filled with automatic rifles, machine guns, flares, and wired canisters that look very much like bombs!

Turn to page 64.

You open the cedar closet door, and Sylvia points toward the secret panel. You deftly pry it open and expose a small red leather box. It is filled with glittering diamonds. One of them, as big as a walnut, seems almost to be giving off its own light!

Sylvia gasps. "The Khartoum Star!"

Grimstone suddenly shoves you aside and grabs the box. "I'll take these and turn them over to the police."

"Wait a minute!" you cry, but Grimstone strides out of the closet, holding the box out of your reach. "Show them out, Kenny!"

"Let me count those diamonds!" you demand.

To your surprise Grimstone turns around and hands you the box. "Go ahead."

You count the diamonds—thirty-seven in all! Grimstone quickly snatches the box and slams it shut.

Suddenly there is a wailing voice—like that of some lost soul who has been stripped of every possession, every friendship, every hope—a wail that grips you with terror! Grimstone clutches the box of diamonds tightly. His hands are shaking.

A whirlwind of white streaking light surrounds you. It closes in as if it's about to squeeze you to death in a coil of ghostly energy.

If you run for the stairs, turn to page 83.

If you stand fast, turn to page 87.

You pull the door open. By the fragrant aroma, you know that you have found the cedar closet! You've almost forgotten about ghosts as you hurry to the back of the closet, if you can call it that—it's as big as a small room. You shine your light on the panel next to the floor at the right rear corner. Kneeling down, you take your pocketknife and insert a blade edge between the floor and the panel. Your heart leaps as the panel flips open. You pull it back and shine your light on a small leather box.

You unlatch the lid and lift it up. The box is filled with diamonds—all glistening and sparkling in the beam of your flashlight!

Then you feel the presence—this time close behind you. You whirl your light around. A sack descends over your head. Powerful hands squeeze your throat. Everything goes black.

The End

60

You rush up to the attic and boldly throw open the door. Before you is a thin, frail figure. His face is pale, and his eyes have a hollow look. He turns and lurches toward you. You start to scream, but stop. It's not a ghost but a live boy—about sixteen, you'd guess. His face has a gentle expression, and he looks more frightened than frightening.

"Please don't tell them about me," he begs.

You step forward to look more closely at this poor tattered figure. "Who are you?"

"My name is Louis. I ran away from home— I've been living here for two months. I make these weird noises to scare people away. If they find out I'm not a ghost they'll kick me out, and I have no other place to stay."

"Hello! Are you up in the attic?" It's Jenny's voice from downstairs. She must have safely gotten off the roof.

"Yes. Come on up!" you call back.

Turning back to Louis, you introduce yourself, but Louis does not offer to shake hands. "Why did you leave home?" you ask. "It must have been pretty bad for you to choose this kind of life."

Turn to page 65.

At this point Chief Ludhorn realizes it is not appropriate for a potential witness to be present at this interrogation and asks you to leave the room. But the next day you lead the police to the attic of Grimstone's house.

While Ludhorn and two officers light up the cedar closet with high intensity flashlights, you pry off a wood panel in the right rear corner.

You can't help being amused by the awed look on the faces of the policemen as you hold a red leather box in front of them and open it. Inside is a collection of sparkling jewels, including one as big as a walnut—the famous Khartoum Star!

The probate court eventually decides that Sylvia Ruston is the rightful owner of the diamonds. As a reward you get one of them and Jenny another. Through questioning Nagar, the police now have enough information to enable them to find Howard Grimstone and the rest of his gang and bring them to justice.

A few weeks later the court orders that Grimstone's house be put up for sale. You wonder who the next owners will be, and whether they will meet Harlowe Thrombey's ghost.

The End

Myra flips the light off and closes the door. "We'd better get back to the kitchen. I wouldn't want to get caught here."

As she is talking, you're eyeing the stairs to the attic. "You go on down," you tell her. "I'll be along in a moment."

Myra looks at you apprehensively. Then, quick and quiet as a cat, she disappears down the stairs. You find your way up two sets of stairs to the attic. As you shine your flashlight around you notice a door. You pull it open. The scent of cedar is unmistakable—you've found the right closet!

Your flashlight beam guides you to a panel in the right rear corner. Wedging the blade of your pocketknife into the crack between the panel and the one next to it, you slowly pry off the unfastened panel. Your eyes rest on a small leather box. Unlatching the lid, you find a large collection of brilliant white diamonds. One of them is larger than you thought a diamond could be. You stare at the sparkling gems in amazement. Sylvia Ruston wasn't kidding!

You're about to put the diamonds in your pockets, but then you stop a second to think. You don't have any right to take the diamonds. You can't be sure who owns them, and you've already taken quite a few risks. Your luck could run out at any time.

If you take the diamonds, turn to page 38.

If you leave them and put back the wood panel, turn to page 100.

Louis suddenly sits down on the floor and leans back against the wall, staring into space. You wonder whether he has forgotten you're there.

"Are you in here?" comes Jenny's voice again. She's at the top of the attic stairs.

"Over here!" you yell, and to Louis you say, "Meet my friend Jenny."

Jenny runs up beside you, stopping short as she spots Louis. "Why, you're not a ghost," she says to him. "But if you don't start eating more you soon will be!"

Louis smiles for the first time and slowly gets to his feet.

"He ran away from home," you explain to Jenny.

"I lived with my uncle," Louis says. "He was drunk a lot, and . . ."

"I bet you'd like a hot bath and a good meal," Jenny says.

"You can come over to my place," you add. "We'll fix you up."

"Thanks. Thanks very much," Louis says. He walks over to the corner of the attic, gathers up some clothes strewn on the floor, and stuffs them in a backpack. Then he follows you and Jenny down the stairs and out of the house.

Turn to page 67.

Flashlight in hand, you climb the broad, carpeted staircase leading to the second story. At the top you face a long hallway with rooms on either side. Halfway down the hall, a short passageway leads to the steps to the third floor. At the top of those steps is a door. You pull it open. Before you are steps leading to the attic. A flick of the switch produces a dim light at the top of the stairs. As you climb the creaky stairs, you glance at your watch. It's eight o'clock now—the hour of the ghost.

A board slips beneath your feet, and you gasp. A few steps further you stop short: Something is moving above you. Then you realize it's only your own shadow, made as you block off light from the passageway below. By the time you reach the top of the stairs you're ready to laugh at yourself for being so jumpy.

Now, shining your flashlight, you walk into the dim, cavernous recesses of the attic. You pass a door. This could be the door to the cedar closet! You're about to open it when a wave of fear runs through your body. You have a strong sensation that someone is nearby, watching you.

You can't see or hear anything, but you feel an overwhelming sense of danger. Then you remember how you felt coming up the stairs— jumping at your own shadow. Maybe you're just nervous, but maybe you've perceived something real.

If you open the door, turn to page 59.

If you pass by the door and circle back down the stairs, turn to page 104.

"Louis, is there anyone else you could live with besides your uncle?" Jenny asks as the three of you walk down the road.

His face brightens for a moment. "My half-brother lives in Alaska. He said I could come up and live with him, but I'd have to raise my own bus fare—and that's a lot of money."

"Maybe so," you say, "but we'll help you find a way."

"You could even join our team of ghost hunters," Jenny says with a laugh. "After all, you've had valuable experience living in that haunted house!"

"I don't know if I want to be a ghost hunter," Louis says. "But I'm pretty good at carpentry."

"Great!" you say. "I know a builder. I'm sure he could use you on his crew."

"Louis," says Jenny emphatically, "you're already halfway to Alaska."

The End

Jenny is eager to help. "I've been thinking about the old Thrombey house since we first talked about it," she says.

It's beginning to get dark that evening as you and Jenny walk along the road that runs past Grimstone's property. In your hand is a rope with a noose at the end, and you have a flashlight in your pocket. You stop at a point opposite the side of the house. "This looks like a good place."

"Okay," Jenny says. "Give me a couple of minutes to get around the corner and start talking to the policeman. That way you can be sure he won't surprise you while you're climbing over the fence."

You wait a short while; then, tossing your rope, you lasso a spike at the top of the fence, and taking up on the rope as you climb, you literally walk up the iron fence.

You teeter at the top a moment, free the noose, and jump down inside the fence. Skirting an empty dog pen, you circle around the back of the house, looking for an unlocked door or window. You don't find any on the first floor, so you climb a cedar tree that's growing close to the rear corner of the house. From the upper branches you're able to reach an unlocked window. It sticks at first, but with an extra shove you get it open. A moment later you're inside an upstairs bathroom.

Turn to page 80.

When you call Grimstone to tell him you're taking the case, he asks you to stop over that evening. You set out for his house right after dinner with your miniature high-intensity flashlight tucked in your pocket. Somehow you think you may need it.

Walking up to the great oak door of the huge Victorian house, you think back to the first time you came here—the night of Harlowe Thrombey's murder. Things have changed a lot since then. A high wrought-iron fence now surrounds the property. Thick cedar hedges have been planted so that it's not possible to see any of the ground-floor windows from the street. The place resembles a fortress more than a gentleman's estate.

As you approach the house, you hear fierce barking. Startled, you turn. For the first time you notice the large dog pen attached to one side of the house. Two huge mastiffs are raging at you from the other side of a chain-link fence. You shudder to think what would happen if they got out.

The front door opens before you reach it. A hulking, square-shouldered man appears. His stiff bristly hair looks like steel wool. A grotesque smile is fixed on his face.

Turn to page 74.

Awful as the rats seem, you're more willing to take your chances with them than to confront the ghost.

"Come on," you say to Jenny.

The two of you strike out through the darkness, hoping the rats will keep clear of you.

One of them runs across your foot. You leap ahead a few feet and feel yourself step on a squishy squirming thing. The rat squeals. Jenny yelps in pain.

"What happened?" you ask.

"I crashed into a wall."

"Sorry. But let's follow the wall. Maybe we'll come to a door."

As you work your way along the wall, another rat brushes your leg. You kick out.

"One of them bit me!" Jenny shrieks.

"Come on, we've got to keep moving!" You hurry on along the wall, feeling for a door.

The rats grow bolder. You feel another . . . another. You jiggle and dance, trying to shove them away.

"Aaaaah!" A rat has bitten you in the calf, right through your jeans! Your whole body shakes.

"I think this is a door!" Jenny yells.

Turn to page 82.

You run down the stairs, practically jumping the last flight. Moments later you rush out of the house, completely forgetting about the policeman on duty. He sees you coming, and he's waiting when you climb over the gate. Jenny has been waiting, too. She runs up behind him.

"What were you doing in there?" the cop demands.

"I saw a ghost. There really is a ghost in there!"

"My friend is a ghost hunter," Jenny puts in.

"Being a ghost hunter gives you no license to trespass on private property. So get in the back seat. I'm going to have to take you down to headquarters and book you."

"I know it's hard to believe," you say, "but there *is* a ghost in there."

"In the car! Now!"

"You'd better not leave till you have a replacement," Jenny says to the policeman.

"Nothing is going to happen in the ten minutes the house is left unguarded!" the cop snaps as you climb into the car.

At that moment a man runs out of the house screaming, *"It's after me! Help!"*

Turn to page 75.

"I hope those dogs can't get out!" you say.

The man laughs. "You don't like our pets? Don't worry—their gate won't open unless we push a button inside the house."

"That's nice to know," you reply, not offering to shake hands. "Is Mr. Grimstone home?"

"Come in, my young friend. Don't be put off by Kenny—he has no manners," Grimstone calls from the foyer.

You walk past Kenny into the great house. It has a much more somber look than you remember. The walls have been covered with dark chestnut paneling. The floors, which used to be polished and shining, are covered with a dark brown stain.

Grimstone shows you into the library. He looks you up and down as if he were measuring you for new clothes. "The ghost starts making noises every night at about eight o'clock. It's almost eight now. I'm going to have to leave you alone for a while. I have to discuss business with my associates in the dining room." Grimstone gives you a funny look. "Do you want to wait here until the noise begins, or do you want to explore the house?"

If you decide to wait in the library, turn to page 46.

If you decide to explore the house, turn to page 106.

"What the—?" In a flash the cop is out of the car—gun drawn.

"It's a ghost—a real ghost!" The man whimpers as he approaches the car.

"See what I mean, officer?" you say.

"Uh-oh," the man exclaims. "Excuse me, I gotta be going."

"Just a minute," says the cop. "Freeze. Raise your hands."

Keeping a bead on the man, the cop reaches inside his car and picks up the radiophone.

"Jorgensen, car six, at the Grimstone house. I've got a man here who may be that suspect for the Union Bank holdup. . . . Yeah, better send a couple of men here."

The cop steps closer to his prisoner. "You're Herman Nagar, aren't you?"

The only response is a muttered curse, which is drowned out by the wail of a police siren.

Looking at you, the cop says, "You can get out. I'm not going to charge you with trespassing, because you helped smoke this man out. But from now on you leave this kind of thing to the police. And you'd better clear out of here before the chief arrives!"

You and Jenny head down the street, trying to decide what to do next.

Turn to page 81.

It's the next day. You're back home, and you're still mad at the way Grimstone treated you. You're trying to figure out what to do next when there's a knock on the door. It's Myra! She rushes inside and slumps exhausted on the couch. You shut the door behind her.

"Hello. You look as if things are going badly," you say.

"I'm really upset," she replies shakily. "Grimstone has gone out of town for two days. When he gets back, I'm going to ask for my pay and quit. I wanted to warn you never to go back there."

"Who's staying at the house now?"

"Just Kenny and Grimstone's poker-playing friends. They're all hit men who wait around doing nothing until a job comes up. When Grimstone goes away they sit up all night playing cards and getting drunk. It frightens me being alone there, but if I walk out now I'll never get my pay back."

A plan is forming in your mind. While Grimstone is away, and with Myra there, you might have a chance to sneak up to the attic and check out the cedar closet.

"Would you mind if I come visit you for a couple of hours tonight?"

Go on to the next page.

"No," says Myra, surprised. "I'd be glad of your company. But you mustn't come to the front door—they'd never let you in. Come around the left side of the house at eight o'clock and tap at the kitchen window. The dogs will be in their pen. Be very quiet so they won't hear you."

After Myra leaves, you reconsider whether you dare undertake your scheme. You have no legal right to search Grimstone's house—and you'll have ferocious dogs, drunken hit men, and crazy Kenny to deal with.

If you go to the house that night, turn to page 57.

If you decide not to risk it, turn to page 88.

You run upstairs and out onto the second-floor porch. Jenny is clinging to the roof, slowly working her way down. The roof is too steep. She slips. She's sliding off the roof! You reach out and grab her wrist. Pulling with all your strength, you lift her up to the porch railing.

"Thanks," Jenny says, shaking, as she slides off the railing and onto the porch. "That face—it was horrible! Please, let's get out of here!"

You and Jenny head back down the hill, happy to have escaped from the Gray mansion alive and sane. You didn't trap a ghost, but at least you found one—or so it seems. And you can consider yourself a fully qualified ghost hunter!

The End

By now it's quite dark in the house. You don't want to attract attention by turning on lights, so you move cautiously along the hallway, shining your flashlight on the floor ahead of you. You look for the stairway to the attic. In a minute you find it.

You're feeling a little scared as you start up the steps. Then you hear laughter coming from the landing above. You stop short. It's a man laughing—and he's laughing at you!

You shine your flashlight up the steps. There is nothing there, and yet there is. The patch of yellow-white light made by your flashlight is forming into a ghost image of a human figure— *Harlowe Thrombey!*

"Who are you? Why are you laughing?" You try to keep your voice from trembling.

"You know who I am. I expected you to save my life, and you didn't. And now I suppose you'd like me to save *your* life?"

"My life doesn't need saving!" you say.

But the only reply you hear is more laughter. Then the image of Harlowe Thrombey disappears, and there is nothing before your eyes but your flashlight beam shining on the wall.

Was Harlowe Thrombey's ghost warning you of some terrible danger, or was he just reminding you that, despite your good intentions, he was murdered?

If you continue on up the attic stairs, turn to page 13.

If you decide it's time to get out of this house, turn to page 72.

From a distance, you and Jenny watch two more police cars converging on the scene. In a few minutes they all pull away.

You can see Nagar sitting alone in the back seat of one of the cars, isolated by wire-mesh grating. He is yelling something at the officers in front. That won't help his case any, you reflect.

"I'm surprised they left the place unguarded," Jenny says.

"I imagine at least one cop will be back soon," you say. "This may be our only chance to get those diamonds!"

"Let's go," says Jenny.

Searching along the perimeter of the house, you find an unlocked kitchen window that you missed last time. It opens with a little prying. You climb inside and give Jenny a hand and pull her in after you. Flashlight in hand, you walk out of the kitchen with Jenny close behind. As you move toward the stairs, you pass by the opulent dining room, where you stop to gaze up at the enormous chandelier from which hang dozens of crystalline lights.

"I think it's swinging a little, Jenny."

"It kind of looks that way," she replies. "But let's just say we're imagining it."

From somewhere above, you hear the ticking of a clock. It grows louder.

"I'm not imagining *that*," you say.

"A ghost clock," Jenny says, and you both laugh.

Turn to page 84.

"Quick, where's the handle?"

"Here!" Jenny pulls and shakes something. The door flies open, letting in a patch of daylight. There's a flight of stone steps ahead. You and Jenny climb the steps. They lead to overhead doors.

Together you raise your hands up against the doors and push. In a moment they swing open. You continue up and out into the rear yard. You're free!

"I've had enough of ghost hunting," Jenny says as you run around the house toward the gate.

"And rat dodging," you add. "We'll have to go to the hospital and get these bites treated."

"Well," says Jenny after you've climbed over the gate and are heading down the street, "maybe we should give up ghost hunting and just stick to murder cases."

"Much more relaxing," you say.

The End

You grab Sylvia's hand and dash for the stairs. As you run through the whirling light your whole body tingles, and for a few moments tiny sparks dance about your clothes as if you're passing through a field of static electricity. As you run, the wailing transforms into cynical laughter.

Still shaking, you and Sylvia rush out the front door, so glad to be alive that for a few moments you completely forget about the diamonds.

But as the two of you walk down the street, your thoughts return once more to your hope of retrieving Sylvia's jewels. There is no point in going back to Grimstone, so the next day you go to the police to tell them what happened.

"Oh, yes," the desk officer says. "Well, I don't know what all that ghost business was about, but Mr. Grimstone came in this morning and turned over a leather box with thirty-seven diamonds—imitation diamonds, that is. One of them was as big as a walnut! Just glass, of course, but very pretty just the same."

The End

The two of you start up the stairs. Almost at once the steps begin to vibrate under your feet. You hear a deep quivering sound. You feel like running, but you force yourself to continue up the stairs. Suddenly, the sound increases in pitch and volume so quickly your hands fly to your ears to cover them. At the same time, a balloon of ghostly white light circles you—narrowing, closing in.

You and Jenny cringe against the stairs. Nothing is touching you, but a tightness in your throat feels like an invisible hand, squeezing your windpipe.

"We've got to get out," Jenny whispers hoarsely.

You feel almost paralyzed, then panicked. You race down the stairs, pulling Jenny along by the hand. Then, as you start down the hall, a terrible thundering noise rumbles along the floor—a sound that could be made by some great boulder tumbling down a mountain.

You open a nearby door and dart in. Jenny is right behind you. She slams the door shut as the thundering noise rolls by. You feel safe for the moment, but you can't even tell where you are. It's pitch-black.

"I've lost my flashlight."

"I have matches," Jenny says.

She lights a match so close under your nose that you rear back from the sulfurous smell. In the brief flickering light you can see you're at the top of a set of stairs leading into a basement.

Go on to the next page.

Jenny shakes out the match to keep from burning her fingers. "I don't want to go down there."

She tries to open the door into the hall, but it's stuck. You grab the doorknob, but your fingers slide off as you push. Your hand is sweating, making the knob slippery.

"Why won't it open?" Jenny cries.

"I think the wood has swollen up. Now we'll *have* to go downstairs."

"I have only a couple of matches left," Jenny says.

"Don't use them yet," you caution.

In darkness, gripping the handrail, you and Jenny start down the steps. The air becomes cooler and damper as you descend.

"This is a deep basement," Jenny says.

"Maybe there's another way out of here," you say hopefully just as you reach the wet cement floor. "It's so deep that ground water must seep in here. Time to light a match."

Jenny strikes a match, but you see only a little flash of light that jumps out from her hand and burns out before it hits the floor.

"The head broke off," Jenny explains. "Only one match left. Oh, I wish I'd brought a candle or something!"

"Might as well light the last match now."

Turn to page 94.

You stand there, faking it—trying to act at ease, when you're actually frightened out of your wits.

Sylvia tugs at your hand. "It's horrible!" She tries to pull you toward the stairs, but you stand your ground, determined not to give in.

The wailing increases in pitch and loudness. Suddenly Kenny bolts. You hear him charging down the stairs like a stampeding bull.

Then you hear a thunk. Grimstone falls to the floor. The noise ends abruptly, and the light begins to fade.

"He's fainted," Sylvia says.

You quickly grab the box of diamonds. "Let's get out of here."

But as you and Sylvia start toward the attic steps, a gray-white figure confronts you. Even in its unformed, shifting state, you recognize it as the ghost of Harlowe Thrombey!

You stop in your tracks, paralyzed by the stare of hollow eyes which emit an energy that penetrates your brain, carrying a message: *Your fate is to be spared this time.*

The image fades into blackness. Grimstone stirs on the floor. You and Sylvia hurry out of the house. Kenny is nowhere to be seen.

A few weeks later, the court rules that Sylvia Ruston is the rightful owner of Jane Thrombey's diamonds—worth $615,000. Sylvia pays you a handsome fee for your help. Later you read that Grimstone has been convicted of a dozen major crimes and sentenced to prison for 199 years.

The End

A few days after your talk with Myra, you stop by the Grimstone house to see if anything is going on. As you stand watching across the street, you are astonished to see furniture being loaded into a van. It looks as if Grimstone and his gang are moving out!

You go back the next day, hoping to get into the empty house. But when you arrive there, you notice a plainclothes detective posted across the street. Returning home, you decide you're not going to be able to accomplish anything on this case without some help. After thinking it over awhile, you pick up the phone and dial Jenny Mudge's number.

Turn to page 68.

You manage to get your head inside the cavity, and you kneel there, panting as you replenish your lungs with fresh air. You never would have guessed that ordinary air could smell and taste so good!

Slowly you feel your head clearing, your energy returning. With renewed fervor you bash away at the sheetrock, opening the hole wider until at last you can crawl through.

You descend the attic stairs cautiously. You hear no signs of life, and indeed you soon find that the house is deserted. Even the dogs are gone. You wonder what happened to the ghost who demanded that you find the diamonds. Suddenly it dawns on you: The ghost that was threatening you must have been a trick of Grimstone's. After he got the diamonds he must have cleared out!

You walk out the door and through the front yard. In a minute you're up over the iron gate and out.

Two men are approaching. They identify themselves as police detectives and take you to headquarters. There you tell Chief Ludhorn of your experience with Howard Grimstone.

"We've been watching the house since he and his men left town yesterday," Ludhorn says "Grimstone was just put on the FBI's most-wanted list. When he's caught—and he will be caught—your testimony will be most helpful in bringing him to justice."

The End

90

Darkness has fallen by the time you reach Mrs. Brewster's house. She greets you excitedly at the door.

"I'm so glad you're here. I didn't dare tell you over the phone why I wanted you to come over so much—you would have thought I had lost my mind."

"Why?"

"The strangest thing has happened. Ziggy—my cat—has come back! Yet I know he was dead. I held his poor lifeless body." Mrs. Brewster steps aside to let you inside and shuts the door behind you.

You give Mrs. Brewster a skeptical look.

"Shh—" Mrs. Brewster puts a finger to her lips. "Listen and you'll hear him."

You hear nothing.

Mrs. Brewster scurries around calling, *"Ziggy . . . Ziggy."* You stand helplessly watching, trying not to laugh, because although you feel sorry for Mrs. Brewster, her behavior is rather comical.

Suddenly she turns to you. "I know he was here. I felt him brush against my leg. I heard him meow. He must have gone out the door when you came in."

"I guess so," you reply. "I hope he comes back again, Mrs. Brewster."

"Oh, I'm sure he will," she calls after you as you hurry down the walk, headed for the cemetery.

Turn to page 116.

You begin your room-by-room search by returning to the library. There, you tap the walls, you check a closet. Nothing unusual. It seems unlikely you'll find any clues before even hearing or seeing any ghosts.

You leave the library and walk down a long dark hallway that leads to a swinging door. Passing through, you find yourself in a pantry lined with cabinets and sinks. You push through another swinging door and find yourself in the huge kitchen, face to face with a young woman dressed in a simple white dress and apron. She jumps back, startled.

"It's all right," you say. "I'm a private detective hired by Mr. Grimstone. I have permission to check through the house."

"Oh," she replies. "I'm Myra, the cook. Why are you checking the house?"

"I'm looking for ghosts. I guess we should hear them pretty soon—it's almost eight."

"Ghosts?" The young woman looks genuinely surprised. "I haven't seen nor heard any ghosts, and I've been living here for almost a month!"

Thinking fast, you realize what has been in the back of your mind all along. There was something fishy about Grimstone's asking you to look for ghosts. It's as if he just invented this to get you over to his house . . . and let you loose in it. But why?

Go on to the next page.

Myra steps closer. "You'd better leave this place. You're only asking for trouble working for Mr. Grimstone."

"What about you? *You're* working for him."

In a hushed voice she says, "I needed a job, and he pays well. But I must leave this place, too—"

"Mr. Grimstone wants you in the library!" It's Kenny, standing in the doorway.

"Be right there." You pull out a notepad, scribble down your name, address, and phone number on a slip of paper, and hand it to Myra. "Call me as soon as you get a chance," you whisper.

By this time Kenny is walking toward you. You stride briskly past him, back to the library. He follows close behind.

In the library, Grimstone wastes no time. "I've decided you don't have it as a ghost hunter," he says. "Now I have other things to do. Kenny will show you out."

You start to argue, but Kenny is hovering over you, looking as if he's itching to pick you up and toss you out the door.

"Better not stick around," Grimstone says. "It's almost time to give the dogs their evening exercise."

Turn to page 76.

This time the match lights up part of the basement, but not enough for you to see where there might be any doors or passageways. What you do see sends a shudder through your bones. Scurrying around the floor are large brown rats—dozens of them! A couple of them are inching closer, as if you've attracted their attention.

"We'd better try that door again." Jenny's voice is shaking as her last match flickers out. The two of you start up the stairs, but you stop short after only a few steps. There's a white glow at the top of the stairs. It expands, lengthening to form a human shape. *You are staring once again at Harlowe Thrombey's ghost.*

"*Oh, no.*" Jenny's voice sounds thin and pinched.

The ghost replies with eerie, echoing peals of laughter.

You stand frozen, more hypnotized than frightened. The ghost neither moves nor talks, but stands motionless, staring at you as if deciding your fate.

"What . . . what can we do?" Jenny squeezes your arm so tightly you almost cry out.

If you continue up the steps toward the ghost, turn to page 37.

If you go back down the steps and grope your way through the basement, looking for steps leading outside the house, turn to page 71.

"Okay, I'll try to find the diamonds," you say.

You come to a door and open it. From the fragrant aroma, you know you've reached the cedar closet. You shine your flashlight around, then step to the right rear corner and pry open the wood panel, revealing a small red leather box.

Suddenly you hear something. You whirl around, half expecting to see a ghost. Instead, you find yourself staring at Howard Grimstone. Kenny, behind him, shines his flashlight in your eyes. Grimstone pushes you aside. You watch with mixed curiosity and fear as he pulls out the leather box and eagerly unlatches it. Inside are dozens of brilliant white diamonds, one of them as big as a walnut!

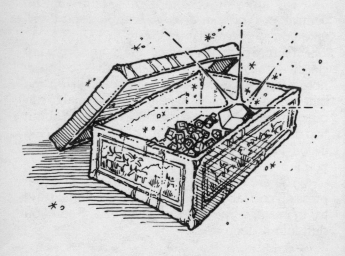

Go on to the next page.

"Very *good*." Grimstone makes a chuckling, rasping sound of contentment. You look around. You want to make a break for it, but Kenny is standing in the closet doorway blocking your escape.

Taking the box, Grimstone replaces the loose panel. Kenny again shines his flashlight in your eyes.

"You've been *very* helpful," Grimstone says, "so we aren't going to kill you. We're going to let you die a natural death."

He waves Kenny and another thug away from the closet doorway then steps outside the closet. You start to follow, but the door slams in your face. You hear the lock turn.

You are a prisoner in a dark room with no ventilation. You can only guess how long it will take you to "die a natural death."

Your prison is bigger than an ordinary closet—really the size of a small room—so you're not in immediate danger of suffocating. On the other hand, you think ruefully, you'll probably run out of oxygen before you starve to death. In about two days, you guess, all the air will be used up. And if you scream and yell and pound on the walls, you'll use it up faster.

You are swept by feelings of anger, then depression and fatigue. Exhausted, you lie down and try to imagine you're somewhere else. Soon you drift into a deep sleep.

Turn to page 101.

The kitchen door closes behind you with a soft click. You stand absolutely still to avoid rousing the dogs while you consider your escape route. The fence is made of shafts of wrought iron. Except at the front gate, where you came in, the crosspieces aren't close enough to serve as rungs on a ladder. But earlier you noticed that in the corner of the yard—out of sight of the dog pen— there is a tree with lower limbs close enough for you to reach. A branch of the tree extends a few feet over the fence. If you can reach that tree, you'll have it made. And your route will be out of sight of the dogs.

Step by step you move across the lawn, hardly daring to breathe. You're a little over half-way to the tree when your right foot brushes against a small rock. Though it makes only the slightest sound, it's enough to bring the dogs to their feet, barking furiously.

You look around. They're coming at you! You break into a mad dash. The dogs are coming fast—closing in! You leap up, grab a branch just above your head, and swing your feet up onto it. You reach for a higher branch and start to pull yourself up.

Turn to page 103.

Leaving the diamonds hidden in their place, you make your way cautiously back down to the kitchen.

Myra is waiting. "Hurry! I overheard Kenny say he's going to turn the dogs loose for the night!"

She lets you out the door. There's no sign of the dogs, so you run straight for the gate. You're about halfway there when you hear furious barking. You know Kenny must be pushing the button that will free the dogs from their pen. Then you hear them baying—charging like a pack of wolves! You run faster than you ever ran before. The dogs are gaining. You grab the gate and climb up and over the top as the dogs leap at you from the other side, growling and barking with rage.

Safe at home again, you decide to stay clear of Grimstone's house for a while. When you get a call from Jenny Mudge a few days later you agree to meet her at the cemetery the following night and do some ghost hunting with her.

Turn to page 110.

You sleep for hours. It may even be the next day when you awake; the air is very stale. You're breathing faster in order to get enough oxygen. You fight back tears as you realize the air isn't going to last as long as you'd hoped. Only then does the thought flash through your mind: You've got to do something. You're fighting for your life!

You rattle the door, jiggle it, shake it. You charge at it, crashing your shoulder against it with as much force as you can bring to bear. The door holds firm.

Then, hardly thinking about what you're doing, you take your pocketknife and pry open the loose panel. Feeling inside, you find a sheetrock wall behind the wood paneling. By wedging your knife under a second panel, you're able to loosen it enough to pry it off with your fingers. You do the same with the third and fourth panels. By now you're gasping for breath from the exertion.

You stop to rest. Somewhat refreshed, you take one of the panels and bash away at the sheetrock wall. But you're feeling dizzy from the bad air. You bend down to keep from fainting. Then you force yourself to straighten up and keep working. If you pass out now, you'll never wake up!

Cocking your arm back, you smash at the sheetrock. Again. With the third stroke you dent it. With the fourth it gives way. A small jagged hole opens. Fresh air!

Turn to page 89.

First thing in the morning, you're on the phone to Sylvia Ruston. "I think I can help you," you say.

"That's wonderful," she replies. "I know it won't be easy getting those diamonds. But you'll be well rewarded."

"I'm glad to hear that; I already have them!"

After explaining to Sylvia everything that happened, you turn the diamonds over to the police. A few days later, they obtain a search warrant based on information you gave them and arrest Grimstone and his gang. A court rules that the diamonds rightfully belong to Sylvia Ruston. She turns over two of them to you as a reward for your good work. She also gives Myra one small diamond and helps her find a new job.

It makes you feel good to have been able to help such a nice person as Sylvia Ruston. And you feel even better when you find out that your new diamonds are worth about $10,000. Not bad, and you've learned not to be afraid of ghosts. In fact, you feel well qualified—if anyone is—to be a full-time ghost hunter!

The End

The dogs are there! One of them lunges, biting you in the left calf. Instinctively you swing back your right foot, striking the dog with enough force in the chest to send it reeling over backward. The other one leaps higher, closing its jaws on your right hip. You hear a ripping sound. It's your jeans! The pocket rips open, spilling out diamonds and loose change.

Suddenly sharp teeth rake your thigh. The other dog! You swing your right leg over a higher branch. Diamonds spill out of your other pocket. You're horizontal—hugging the branch—just out of reach of the leaping dogs. You manage to get a good grip on a higher branch and pull yourself up to a standing position. You work your way to the big limb overhanging the fence, crawl along it, and drop to safety on the other side of the fence.

You can hear men yelling in the yard, but you're already running around the corner and through someone's yard.

Turn to page 3.

104

You walk past the cedar closet. If someone is watching, you don't want them to see where the diamonds are hidden!

You're feeling increasingly nervous. In fact, you'd like to get out of this house as fast as possible. You quicken your step and start down the stairs. Your flashlight beam falls on a picture hung on the wall.

Wait! There's something strange about that picture. People don't usually hang pictures by the attic stairs. You pull the picture away from the wall and find a loudspeaker! As you put the picture back on the wall, a wailing, moaning sound—like the anguished cry of a ghost—blasts in your ears. The sound is clearly coming from the speaker. This ghost is a tape recording!

Turn to page 115.

"I'd just as soon get started exploring the house," you say.

"That's perfectly fine," Grimstone replies pleasantly—too pleasantly. "You can go any-where—we have no secrets here."

As the two of you walk through the down-stairs hall, he motions to the dining room, where Kenny and three other men are seated at the dining-room table. "Excuse me, I have some busi-ness to conduct with these gentlemen." He enters the dining room, closing the door behind him.

You stand in the hallway a moment, thinking. Everything about Grimstone—his thuggish lackey, the high iron fence outside, the huge guard dogs—all confirm Sylvia's opinion of him as a pro-fessional criminal. Yet he's given you the run of the house to look for ghosts. It's odd.

You'd like to find evidence of ghosts, but to tell the truth, you're even more curious to find out whether Jane Thrombey's diamonds are hidden in the attic cedar closet. This may be your only chance—while no one is watching you.

If you decide to go directly to the attic and search the cedar closet, turn to page 66.

If you decide to explore the house room by room, working your way up to the attic, turn to page 92.

"Look, wait a second! I'll talk," you plead. "I handed the diamonds over to the police."

Kenny slaps you hard across the face. You go reeling across the room.

"Don't give us that!" Grimstone barks. "If you had done that, the police would have let me know. After all, you stole the diamonds from my house."

You cringe against the bookcase as Grimstone towers over you, his forefinger planted on your cheekbone, just below your right eye.

"Help! Please!" you cry out.

The thugs laugh and Grimstone breaks into a broad smile. "*Help?*" he says, mocking you. "This is a soundproof room, kid. No one can help you here."

The moment Grimstone utters these words, the lights flicker violently and the house begins to shake.

"Boss, what's going on?" Kenny yells.

Grimstone looks helplessly around. "Herman, check the basement. Maybe something is wrong with the furnace."

One of the thugs rushes out of the room. You work your way along the bookcase. Grimstone starts after you, but his way seems blocked by a whirling white shape that sends out a shower of silvery sparks. Grimstone, Kenny, and the other thugs retreat to the far wall. They huddle paralyzed with terror as the whirling white blur comes to a rest and turns into the ghost image of Harlowe Thrombey!

Turn to page 114.

You make a break for it, throw open the window, and swing yourself through feet first. Someone lunges after you as you jump onto the slanting roof.

When you hit, your momentum carries you along—you can't stop! At the edge of the roof you have to jump. Screaming, you leap toward a cedar tree growing close to the house. It helps break your fall, but you are thrown sideways. Your head bangs against a rock as you hit ground, and you're out cold.

You wake up in a hospital bed—your aching head bandaged and your right leg in a cast. Your scream saved your life. A patrolman was at your side even before Grimstone got out of the house to look for you. The police had been suspicious of Grimstone and were keeping an eye on his house.

The doctor says you'll be in the hospital for a week and on crutches for two months after that. You won't be hunting any ghosts for a while.

The End

After hanging up the phone, you glance at the calendar. It shows the moon will be full tomorrow night. What better time for ghost hunting! You shudder at the thought of going to the cemetery, but if that's what it takes to find a ghost, you'll have to do it!

The next day the weather turns cold and windy. Dark clouds race across the sky. You wonder whether the full moon will even be visible.

Just as it's getting dark the phone rings. It's Mrs. Brewster, an elderly woman who lives near the cemetery. You've heard about her—she seems to know everyone in town.

"You're a detective, aren't you?" she begins.

"Well . . . yes."

"Good, then I have a case for you. My cat, Ziggy, died last week, and the vet says that he might have been poisoned. I want to find out who did it. It's important I see you right away. Could you please come over?"

*If you agree to stop by Mrs. Brewster's,
turn to page 90.*

*If you tell her you're sorry but you're busy this
evening, go on to the next page.*

You reach the cemetery just as the full moon breaks out from behind a cloud. The moonlight flickers through the trees as their branches swing back and forth in the wind. Patches of light and shadow dance about the gravestones.

Suddenly the moon passes behind a cloud. You feel something brush against your neck—it's a falling leaf.

A scream cuts the air! You turn and see a figure that suddenly fades from view as the moon again slips behind a cloud. There's no doubt in your mind: It's a ghost!

Summoning your courage, you advance, step by step, toward the place where you saw the fleeting image.

The moon reappears, shining fully on the approaching figure.

"Jenny!" you call.

"I thought you were a ghost!" she says.

"I was hunting for ghosts, but I'm glad I found you instead."

"Same here," says Jenny. "As soon as I got here I almost tripped over a black cat, and then you scared me to death."

"If I scared you to death, you must be a ghost yourself!" you reply.

Laughing, the two of you head back to Jenny's house for cider and doughnuts.

All the way there you wonder about the cat Jenny saw in the cemetery. Could it have been Ziggy? If it was, then Jenny saw a ghost without realizing it. Too bad, you'll never know.

The End

You dash out of the attic, down the stairs. You whip around a corner and trip over a small black box. Sparks jump out. You see another of Grimstone's thugs; he yells at you, cursing. You're on your feet and running down the next flight of stairs. You leap the last five steps and race down the hallway. At that moment an explosion sends a blast and a series of shock waves through the house.

Shaken, and deafened from the noise, you race for the front door, wondering what happened. Grimstone's man must have been making a bomb and somehow you triggered it when you tripped over it. As you reach the door you hear a rapid series of explosions coming from the rear of the house—it's as if an ammunition dump is going off! The blasts virtually blow you out the front door. But you're not hurt, and in a few moments you're over the gate. You cross the street and lean up against a stone wall, grateful to be alive and free.

By now flames are shooting through a blown-out section of the roof. You hear fire engines a few blocks away. One of Grimstone's men hobbles out of the house, his shirt ripped open, face blackened with soot. By the time he reaches the gate, two police cars have arrived. The first two fire engines pull up by the front gate. But with a huge cache of explosives fueling the flames, it's obvious the house will be a total loss, and the diamonds, no doubt, as well.

The End

You stroll over to a desk and pick up the phone. "Give me the police. This is an emergency!"

Harlowe Thrombey's ghost whirls around the room like a tornado. Grimstone and his men cringe by the couch. You watch calmly. A few minutes later the police burst into the house. At that same moment, the ghost disappears. Grimstone starts toward you, but two police officers are already in the room. They grab him, one by each arm.

Shortly afterward Chief Ludhorn arrives. You show him the cache of weapons, and Grimstone's fate is sealed. He and his henchmen are carted off to jail. The dogs are sent to the pound, and the house is locked up.

Early the next morning, you climb over Grimstone's gate. After an hour of searching, you manage to find all thirty-seven of the lost diamonds. You turn them over to the police, and a few weeks later a court rules that Sylvia Ruston is the rightful owner of the diamonds.

You wonder whether you'll be able to charge Sylvia a fee for your services. After all, you never actually did agree to take the case.

Sylvia Ruston, you find, is a very fair-minded woman. She gives you two of the diamonds as a reward. You take them to a jeweler and find that the smaller one is worth $5,500. The larger one, being somewhat less pure and brilliant, is worth only $4,500. Still, not bad.

The End

You race down the stairs and find Grimstone waiting in the downstairs hall.

"Well, did you find any ghosts?" he demands.

"It's a *modern* ghost you have here, Mr. Grimstone, recorded on tape."

"You're a smart little devil."

"Thanks for your compliment. I must be on my way," you say airily.

As you are speaking you hear someone behind you. It's Kenny. You feel sure he was following you all along—that Grimstone was hoping you would give away the location of the diamonds. He obviously concocted the ghost business to entice you into searching the house!

"Shall we make a ghost out of this kid?" Kenny asks, a terrible leer on his stubbly face.

"Shut up!" Grimstone snarls. "Show the kid out."

Kenny holds the door for you, and you waste no time on further goodbyes.

You've found no ghost, but you've solved a mystery of sorts. And you're still alive and well, which is a pretty good accomplishment for anyone who has had dealings with Howard Grimstone.

The End

You reach the cemetery shortly after dark, just as the full moon breaks out from behind a cloud. The moonlight flickers through the trees as their branches swing back and forth in the wind. Patches of light and shadow dance among the gravestones.

Go on to the next page.

You stop, startled, as something—a small animal—runs from behind a bush and disappears behind a large tombstone. You climb up on the base of the tombstone and peer over the top.

Looking up at you is a large black cat with a white-tipped tail. You grab it and look at the tag fastened to its collar. By the light of the moon you can read the name—*ZIGGY*. Suddenly the cat leaps out of your arms. As you stand up to see where it runs, a scream cuts the air.

Turning, you see a figure that fades from view as the moon slips behind a cloud. There's no doubt in your mind—it's a ghost!

The moon returns, shining dimly through a veil of clouds on the figure walking toward you—

"Jenny!" you call.

She runs up. "Oh, I thought you were a ghost!"

"I was hunting ghosts," you say, "but I'm glad I found you instead."

"Same here," says Jenny. "I've had enough of this business for tonight. I stopped by Mrs. Brewster's house. Her cat died last week and she claims the cat's ghost is haunting her house. What a silly woman."

"What was the cat's name?" you ask.

Jenny looks puzzled. "Why, I don't remember. Oh, yes, now I do—it was Ziggy."

"Guess what, Jenny?" you say. "I think I caught a ghost tonight."

The End

ABOUT THE AUTHOR

EDWARD PACKARD is a graduate of Princeton University and Columbia Law School. He developed the unique storytelling approach used in the Choose Your Own Adventure series while thinking up stories for his children, Caroline, Andrea, and Wells.

ABOUT THE ILLUSTRATOR

TED ENIK is the illustrator of the Sherluck Bones Mystery-Detective books, which were written by Jim and Mary Razzi and published by Bantam Books. He has also illustrated *The Curse of Batterslea Hall* in Bantam's Choose Your Own Adventure series. In the Bantam Skylark Choose Your Own Adventure series, he has illustrated *The Creature from Miller's Pond, Summer Camp, The Mummy's Tomb, Ice Cave,* and *Runaway Spaceship.* Mr. Enik lives in New York City.